PETER'S CAT

PETER'S CAT

by

Steve English

solway

First published 1996 by Solway

02 01 00 99 98 97 96   7 6 5 4 3 2 1

Solway in an imprint of Paternoster Publishing,
P.O. Box 300, Carlisle, Cumbria CA3 0QS

British Library Cataloguing in Publication Data

A catalogue record for this book is available from the British Library.

p/b ISBN 1–900507–17–x
h/b ISBN 1–900507–30–7

Printed in Great Britain by
The Guernsey Press Co Ltd, Vale, Guernsey, Channel Islands.

FOR MY NEVER-TO-BE-AGED P's.

THE CAT SAT ON MATT.

Now there was a man of the
Pharisees named Nicodemus. . . . He
came to Jesus by night.

The wind blows wherever it pleases. You hear its sound but you cannot tell where it comes from or where it is going.

A PROVERB

Better to live on a corner of the roof than share a house with a quarrelsome wife.

Watch out for false prophets. They come to you in sheep's clothing, but inwardly they are ferocious wolves.

Luke 8:22-25

HELLO THERE ZEALOT. CHEWED THE BONES OF ANY ROMANS LATELY?

YEAH, AND IF YOU DON'T STOP PESTERING ME I'LL BITE YOUR HEAD OFF IN ONE GO!

CHOKE, SPLUTTER, SORRY FOR OPENING MY MOUTH. I'LL JUST BE ON MY WAY SHALL I?

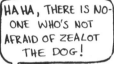

HA HA, THERE IS NO-ONE WHO'S NOT AFRAID OF ZEALOT THE DOG!

SPLUTTER, YOU KNOW ZEALOT'S BARK IS WORSE THAN HIS BITE BUT HIS BREATH IS WORSE THAN THOSE TWO PUT TOGETHER!

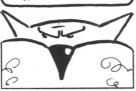

"...HIDE ME IN THE SHADOW OF YOUR WINGS"

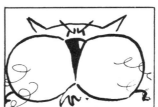

Matthew 6:17

But when you fast, put oil on your head and wash your face, so that it will not be obvious to men that you are fasting.

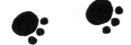

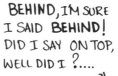

A PROVERB

Like one who seizes a dog by the ears is a passer-by who meddles in a quarrel not his own.

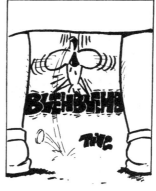

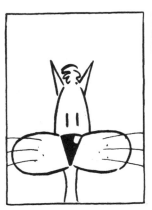

A PROVERB

Do not love sleep or you will grow poor; stay awake and you will have food to spare.

John 1:42

BUT A SAMARITAN, AS HE
TRAVELLED, CAME WHERE
THE MAN WAS; AND WHEN HE
SAW HIM, HE TOOK PITY ON HIM.

THEN WENT TO HIM AND
BANDAGED HIS WOUNDS,

POURING ON OIL AND WINE.

SPLOSH

THEN HE PUT THE MAN ON HIS
OWN DONKEY, BROUGHT HIM TO
AN INN AND TOOK CARE OF
HIM.

OUR BUDGET FOR
THIS PRODUCTION
DIDN'T QUITE
STRETCH TO A
DONKEY!

THE NEXT DAY HE TOOK OUT TWO SILVER COINS, AND GAVE THEM TO THE INNKEEPER.

"LOOK AFTER HIM," HE SAID, "AND WHEN I RETURN I WILL REIMBURSE YOU FOR ANY EXTRA EXPENSE YOU MAY HAVE."

I'VE DECIDED TO BECOME A RECLUSE!

Mark 7:9

AND THE LION LAY DOWN WITH THE LAMB.

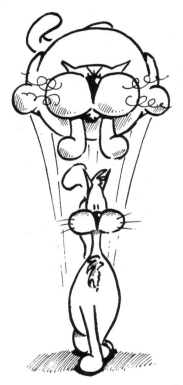

WELL PHARISEE'S CAT, WE'VE DECIDED THAT YOU ARE A BIT OF A..... WHAT'S THAT WORD?.... A HIPPOCAT!

DON'T YOU MEAN HYPOCRITE?

DO WE?

NO, I MEANT WHAT I SAID THE FIRST TIME.

JERUSALEM

A PROVERB

A prudent man sees danger and takes refuge, but the simple keep going and suffer for it.

A PROVERB

A fool's talk brings a rod to his back...

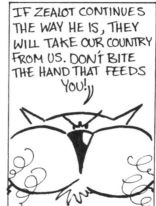

A PROVERB

Even a fool is thought wise if he keeps silent, and discerning if he holds his tongue

Now that I, your Lord and Teacher, have washed your feet, you also should wash one another's feet.

SABBATH IN AN UPPER ROOM.

SABBATH IN THE DEPTHS

HA HA WE'VE GOT HIM

BUT IT'S GETTING RATHER CHILLY IN HERE HAS SOMEONE LEFT THE DOOR OPEN?

EXCUSE ME SIRE, IT'S ABOUT OUR NEW ARRIVAL

∨

YES I KNOW WHO HE IS DID HE ARRIVE KICKING AND SCREAMING LIKE THE REST OF THEM?

WELL THAT'S THE PROBLEM! YOU SEE HE KICKED OUR FRONT GATES IN, AND EM.... PEOPLE ARE LEAVING....!

John 20:3,4

So Peter and the other disciple started for the tomb. Both were running, but the other disciple outran Peter and reached the tomb first.

Then Simon Peter, who was behind him arrived and went into the tomb.

A PROVERB

There is no wisdom, no insight, no plan that can succeed against the Lord.

John 21:7-11

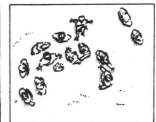

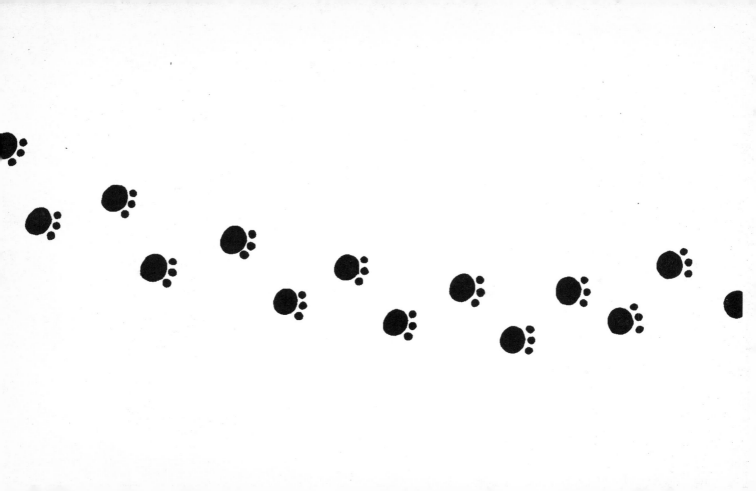